THE DEATH OF DR. DEAN

THE DEATH OF DR. DEAN

A Novella By

JACK COEY

Adelaide Books
New York / Lisbon

2018

The Death of Dr. Dean
a novella by Jack Coey

Copyright © 2018 By Jack Coey
Cover image © 2018 Adelaide Books

Published by Adelaide Books, New York / Lisbon
An imprint of the Istina Group DBA
adelaidebooks.org

Editor-in-Chief
Stevan V. Nikolic

For any information, please contact Adelaide Books
at info@adelaidebooks.org

ISBN13: 978-0-9996451-5-4
ISBN10: 0-9996451-5-3

Printed in the United States of America

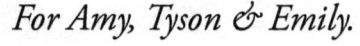

For Amy, Tyson & Emily.

Prologue

Charles Rich and William Dean were friends for over twenty years. They were intelligent, well-educated men in a small farming community named Jaffrey NH. on the Massachusetts' border. William was called Doctor, although trained as a doctor, he never practiced. He lived with his wife, Mary, on a hilltop farm two miles out of the village of Jaffrey. Dr. Dean had a spectacular view of Mount Monadnock, and he milked his cows late in the morning, and late at night, and after his body was found stuffed down a well, it was thought he had information about the lights that someone didn't want him to share with The Department of Justice. People saw lights from the mountain beginning in the summer of 1916, and it was feared there were German spies signaling boats in the ocean sixty miles away about troop movements from Fort Devens. The Department of Justice sent agents to Peterborough NH in April of 1918 to investigate the lights under The Espionage Act of 1917. On the morning of August 14, 1918 Dr. Dean's body was found in a well at the same time his good friend showed up with a black eye.

Chapter One

On August 13th, Dr. Dean woke mid-morning, and was visited by three women who were looking for donations for a rummage sale to be held to raise money to build a hospital in Peterborough. Mrs. Morison of Peterborough, and Miss Harrington and Mrs. Lynch called on Dr. and Mrs. Dean to ask for articles to be auctioned off. Mrs. Morison was involved with the lights, and had spoken to The Department of Justice in Boston to have agents travel to Peterborough to investigate; had the agents staying on her farm, and using her telescope in the library to watch for lights.

Later in the day, after the women had left, Dr. Dean made a trip to the village. Tuesday was the day of the week the shops in the village stayed open late so the farmers could stay in their fields until dusk and still be able to shop. Dr. Dean made weekly trips to the village for supplies, and since his wife was suffering from senile dementia, he made the trips alone. One characteristic Charles Rich and Dr. Dean shared was they enjoyed the company of women. Mr. Rich, because of his position in town, had to be more discreet. He was the head cashier at the bank, moderator of the town meeting, former senator and representative to the house, treasurer for the school, National Guard, and choir director of the church, municipal judge, and a Mason. Charles Rich said Dr. Dean came to visit him that night just after he'd been kicked by his horse, but Mrs. Dean told investigators her husband returned to the farm at nine thirty which made implausible Rich's assertion that he was at Rich's house at ten after nine. Rich told others Mrs. Dean was mentally unstable and was not reliable. Dr. Dean returned to his farm changed into his work clothes, had a muffin to eat, and went to the barn to milk the cow. Mrs. Dean cooked soup waiting for his return. The longer he was late, the more anxious she became. She dosed on and off all night, and at first light, went to the barn, and found his lantern overturned. She called out to him and was answered by silence.

Arthur Smith was a twenty-one year old farm hand on loan to Dr. Dean to do some mowing, coming onto the farm for the second day, the 14th, with his boss's six-year old son Josh Ingraham. He drove the buggy up the farm road to where he stopped yesterday. He was changing over the horse from the buggy to the mowing machine when he heard a scream. He jerked up, and saw Mrs. Dean clumsily running across the field. He ran towards her.

"Dr. Dean is dead in the barn! Please go look!" she screamed. He was momentarily stunned, and went back to Josh, and told him to stay where he was, and ran to the barn. He pushed open the sliding door, and looked around the main floor before climbing the ladder to the hayloft. He came back down and went outside. He walked to where Mrs. Dean was, and said,

"He's not there."

Mrs. Dean, in an agitated state, told Arthur how Dr. Dean went to the village in the late afternoon, and came home at nine thirty, and went out to do his milking, and never came back. She came out at first light to look for him, but didn't find him, and thought he died. As she was talking, Arthur saw a wagon come up the road with a man and boy in it who, as they got closer, he recognized as Matt Garfield and his son.

Garfield and his son got down from the wagon, and walked over to where Arthur and Mrs. Dean were. Garfield's son was thirteen or so. Mrs. Dean went over her story again how her husband came home at nine thirty, and went out to the barn at eleven to milk the cow, and never came back. She said she was up most of the night, and came out at dawn to look for him in the barn, and couldn't find him. She called out to him, and when he didn't answer, she thought he was dead. Garfield wasn't so sure about that. She was emotionally wrought and suffered from dementia besides and who would kill Dr. Dean? Garfield thought Dr. Dean wandered off somewheres and was lying injured. He was patient with Mrs. Dean, and when she finished, he said,

"Let's have a look around."

Garfield walked Mrs. Dean back to the bungalow. There were three buildings on the farm: the bungalow where the Deans moved from the big house after they rented the big house to the Colfelts from New York City. The bungalow was on the left as you came up the farm road from the town road, and across the field from that was the barn, and at the top of the hill with spectacular views of

Monadnock is the big house. The big house was still empty since the Colfelts left in June. The men and boys split into two groups and went over the fields, and joined back up together by the big house. Garfield's son tried the door and windows and everything was locked, that is, until he found an unlocked window by the front door. He crawled through, and opened the door for the other three.

Chapter Two

People began seeing lights from the mountain during the summer of 1916 at the same time the Colfelts – Lawrence and Margaret came to Jaffrey. They rented a house in Jaffrey at that time with the explanation that they wanted to be near their daughter, Natalye, who was at college at Radcliffe. The Colfelts had money. The Deans were struggling on the farm to make money, and it was Charles Rich's idea to have the Deans rent out the big house to make money. The Colfelts went back to New York at the end of 1916 season, and showed up again in August of 1917, looking for a house to rent. The Deans agreed to rent to the Colfelts which was a bad decision. Dr. Dean and Mary had been on the farm for twenty years by themselves, and to have tenants was an imposition especially tenants like the Colfelts who hired domestic help while the Deans were struggling. There was the feeling of "work or fight" for able-bodied men and Colfelt didn't work which made the natives suspicious. He rode horses or drove around in his Marmon touring car, and displayed a haughty attitude toward the locals which exacerbated the negative feelings about him.

The four were in the house, and the first thing they noticed was how cluttered it was with articles left by the Colfelts.

The Colfelts moved out the first week of June, 1918 under unclear circumstances. It was obvious they didn't mind leaving a mess for Dr. Dean. The house was musty and echoed as the group moved around. They looked through both floors: no Dr. Dean.

When they came out of the house, they split up in different directions, and Garfield walked back to the barn, and sat on the porch. He wiped his forehead with a handkerchief. He looked at the mountain, and remembered his friend telling him about a cave off the Pumpelly trail where the German spies were. Josh Ingraham came and sat next to him. They looked down at the grass, and saw blood stains, and Josh reached down, and plucked a blade of grass, and asked,

"What's this?"

Garfield had apprehensions but made light of them.

"Looks like Dr. Dean killed a chicken or something," he told the boy. Garfield saw more blood in the grass, and knew something happened here. He decided to call down to the village. He told Josh he wanted to use the telephone, and they walked back to the big house. Garfield went inside the house, and told the operator he wanted to speak with Selectman Coolidge. When Coolidge came on the line, Garfield told him how Dr. Dean was missing since last night, and Coolidge answered he would round up some men, and be there as soon as he could.

Chapter Three

It was a little after ten in the morning when the automobile came up the farm road, and stopped near the bungalow. Selectman Coolidge, Selectman Hogan, and Charlie Nute, the Chief of Police, got out, and walked up to the big house where they met the four on the porch. Garfield told the officials how Dr. Dean went to the village last night, came home, and went out to the barn to milk the cow, and never came back. Garfield said they searched the fields and barn and big house.

"No sign of him anywhere, eh?" asked Charlie Nute.

"He's hurt lying somewheres," offered Arthur.

"I've come across something down here," said Garfield. Garfield told the boys to stay on the porch, and led the men down by the porch, and showed them the blood stains.

"Oh! This doesn't look good," said Nute.

The blood entertained the possibility of a crime, and the men became more urgent. They walked over to the bungalow, and were searching around the bungalow, when Hogan came across a well. He called to the other men, and slid the cover off, and looked down into it, and saw it was empty.

"Any other wells on the place?" he asked.

"There's one by the big house," answered Garfield.

The men walked up to the big house, and found the well next to the foundation. Coolidge took the cover off, and looked down into it.

"There's water in this one. Can I get a pole to poke around with?"

Garfield went into the big house, and came out with a broom, and handed it to Coolidge. Coolidge straddled the well, and plunged the handle down into it, and moved it around, and said,

"He's here all right."

The men were stunned. They froze until Coolidge said,

"If I can get a hook of some kind, I'll pull him up."

Coolidge's face was sweaty and white.

"There's an ice pick in the barn," said Arthur.

"Yes, that should work," said Coolidge.

Arthur headed for the barn, and saw an auto coming up the farm road. The auto drove up to the big house and parked and Mutt Priest and Charlie Stratton got out. They saw from the expression on the men's faces something serious was going on. Stratton said Mrs. Dean called them about the livestock. After a few more minutes, Arthur returned with the ice pick which he handed to a morose Coolidge.

"Looks like Mrs. Dean is coming," said Mutt Priest.

The men saw Mrs. Dean coming after hearing the auto go by the bungalow and Coolidge said,

"You fellows look after this, and I'll take the boys, and see that Mrs. Dean doesn't come up here."

He handed the ice pick to Stratton, and headed off with

the boys. Stratton got down in the well, and dropped the pick, and pulled up. The men saw a pair of legs with rope wrapped around the knees.

"Oh My God!" someone said.

"Let him down," ordered Hogan.

The men froze and an agitated Hogan paced back and forth.

"State law says we have to call the county coroner before we move the body," sternly stated Hogan, "don't do anything further until you're told to do so."

Abruptly, he walked off looking for Coolidge who was the chairman of the selectmen. Hogan found him in the barn with the boys and Mrs. Dean feeding turkeys. Hogan reminded Coolidge he had to call the coroner. As he walked across the field to the bungalow, Coolidge had the idea to call up Charles Rich who was a good friend of Dr. Dean's, and his wife, to come up and be with Mrs. Dean. They could distract Mrs. Dean while they took her husband's body out of the well. When he got inside the bungalow, he picked up the receiver, and out the window saw an auto park near the bungalow. Will Leighton, the undertaker, and Charles Rich, and his wife, Lana, and sister-in-law, Georgiana Hodgkins, got out. He thought,

"How does anyone know we need an undertaker when no one knows he's dead yet?"

Chapter Four

The Riches and undertaker walked up the road to the big house where the men were waiting. They all saw the black eye. It was unusual for a man of Charles Rich's stature to have a black eye like a priest or schoolteacher or doctor. No one asked him about it because of the urgency of the body in the well, and one didn't trifle with Charles Rich. Rich was standing at the side of the well, and Garfield said,

"We've found him here in the well."

"I guess it's a case of suicide, isn't it?" suggested Rich.

"I don't think so," countered Garfield, "how can a man tie his knees, and pull the cover over him at the same time he's drowning? If you would like to see him, we could have him drawn up again."

"No, I don't care to see him."

The sky was getting dark, and it was just after two when an automobile came up the road. Dr. Dinsmoor, the county medical examiner, and Roy Pickard, the county attorney, got out of the auto. Coolidge told the men Dr. Dean went to the village the night before, came home, and went to the barn to milk, and never came back. They found his body in the well. There was a storm coming so Dr. Dinsmoor, Mr. Leighton, and Selectman Coolidge were around the well, and Coolidge hooked the body with the pick, and when he pulled up, Dr. Dinsmoor embraced the corpse, and pulled it out of the well. He laid the corpse on the ground. Dr. Dean's hands were tied behind his back, and a rope was wound around his neck and knees, and there was a sack pulled over his head. The men were shocked at the grisly discovery. Dr. Dinsmoor took out a pocket knife, and cut away the sack, and discovered a medium-sized stone.

"Save everything as evidence," ordered Roy Pickard.

There was a horse blanket wrapped around Dr. Dean's head which when removed revealed three gashes on the victim's forehead. It started to rain.

"Help me move the body into the house," asked Leighton. A couple of men stepped forward, and helped carry the corpse into the big house. They laid him on the parlor floor. A half hour later there was a full-blown storm with heavy rain and strong winds which destroyed much of the outside evidence.

Chapter Five

From The Department of Justice report of April 15, 1918:

After reviewing the data this far collected by Operative Valkenburgh it appeared to all at the conference that there was considerable likelihood that some system of communication by lights was being at least experimented upon in southern New Hampshire inasmuch as several lights have been positively seen, and do not appear to be due to any natural causes.

Robert Valkenburgh and Feri Weiss were two Department of Justice agents who traveled by train from Boston to Peterborough, NH. in April of 1918 to investigate the reports of lights from Mount Monadnock. In June of 1917, congress passed The Espionage Act of 1917 which stated that any aid or comfort to the enemy was subject to fines or imprisonment, and The Department of Justice had reports from the Monadnock region of German spies signaling boats in the ocean from the summit of Monadnock. The Germans were following troop movements from Fort Devens. Mrs. Horace Morison was involved in watching for signal lights, and she requested to Boston to send agents. It only took her a few days to find Valkenburgh and Weiss after they arrived in Peterborough, and had them move to her house so they could watch for lights with the telescope in her library. They had rooms on the third floor servants' quarters, and ate most of their meals in the kitchen with the domestic help. After dark, Valkenburgh and Weiss would man the telescope, and watch. One night late, Valkenburgh grunted. Weiss lay on the couch reading The Police Gazette.

"Feri, I see something."

"Yeah?"

"It's a moving, swinging light. Oh! Now it's swinging."

"What's the location?"

There was a pause.

"Northeast. I would guess half a mile, but that's a guess."

"Sure. We'll check it out in the morning."

After several minutes.

"Ah! It's moving and swinging again."

"Probably a lantern..."

"Now it stopped and is swinging."

"Is it elevated?"

"Naw."

"Probably a lantern..."

"I'm not so sure..."

"Bob, how can you signal the Atlantic from here standing at ground level?"

"They only have one operation?"

"I hadn't thought of that. But I'm too tired to think about that now. Let's hit the hay, and tomorrow's another day."

Chapter Six

From The Department of Justice report of April 28, 1918:

Continuing investigation previously reported April 27, after a late breakfast, Agent helped Mrs. Morison with her house work and in her garden. After lunch, Agent inspected her farm, and prepared supper for her in time for her to take the 6:22 P.M. train from Noone Station.

During the summer of 1916 – the summer the lights first appeared, Johann Von Bernstorff, the German ambassador to The United States, made two trips to Dublin, NH. the next town to Jaffrey. Domestic help and chauffeurs told Valkenburgh and Weiss he was in the company of other men, and meetings were held in cabins, and on out-of-the way picnics. There were women during the off-hours. This was when the Colfelts showed up in Jaffrey, and rented a house. They returned to New York City at the end of the season, and returned to Jaffrey in August of 1917. Charles Rich suggested they rent the big house on Dean farm. Dr. Dean wasn't happy about sharing his farm, but given the financial situation, he couldn't very well refuse. Dr. Dean and Colfelt didn't get along from the start. Colfelt didn't work which angered Dean because he was working to stay on his farm. Colfelt hired cooks and gardeners while Dean did all the work himself. Mrs. Dean was losing capacity so more of the responsibility was falling to her husband. Other farmers who knew Dean's predicament would loan him workers like Arthur Smith to help out. Colfelt's haughty attitude didn't help matters either both with Dean and the locals. Given Colfelt's disdain, it was seen as odd that the Colfelts would spend the winter of 17-18 on Dean farm when they had the capacity to go anywhere they wanted. In the spring of 1918, Valkenburgh and Weiss asked Dr. Dean about Colfelt because they had information he was the illegitimate son of Johann Von Bernstorff, and he answered,

"He's one hundred percent American."

Although by June of 1918, Dr. Dean gave the Colfelts twenty-four hours to vacate his farm which explains why there was so much stuff left in the big house. Pete Hamill, the village blacksmith, and some of his employees, helped Colfelt move to a hill-top house in Temple. One of last articles to move was a wooden box that was on the porch of the big house. Two men went to lift it, and they could barely move it. Colfelt told them it was a victrola and he was fussy about how it was handled. It took three men to slide it onto the back of the truck. Hamill thought,

"If this is a victrola, then, I'm Babe Ruth." He'd heard the rumors about Colfelt's sympathies for the Germans, and couldn't help but think, if it was a signaling device of some kind.

Chapter Seven

It was the morning of August 13, 1918 that Mrs. Morison visited Dean farm. She was with two other women. The women got out of their auto around mid-morning and walked to the bungalow. Mrs. Morison knocked on the screen door, and Mrs. Dean came to the opening. Mrs. Morison saw the food stains on her dress. Mrs. Dean thought they were religious people, and when Mrs. Morison tried to tell her why they were there, it only confused her. Exasperated, Mrs. Dean invited the women into the bungalow. The women were awkwardly standing in the middle of a somewhat shabby sitting room when Dr. Dean came down the stairs. Mrs. Morison thought this was rather late for a farmer to be starting his day. Dr. Dean was surprised and pleased to see the women. Mrs. Morison told him why they were there, and he enthusiastically responded. He said he had a painting he could donate, and he went out of the room to look for it. He came back several minutes later, and said it must be in the big house, and invited the ladies to walk with him up to the big house. Mrs. Morison could see the other women didn't want to go so she offered to go. Dr. Dean and Mrs. Morison walked up the road to the big house. He unlocked the front door, they went inside, and there were boxes and articles strewn all over the place.

"Please overlook the mess," said Dr. Dean, "you wouldn't think the Colfelts would behave like this."

She stood while he looked around the rooms, and then, he climbed the stairs to the second floor, and she heard echoes in the musty house. He came down the stairs carrying a spinning wheel.

"Oh, Dr. Dean are you sure you want to donate something that valuable?" asked Mrs. Morison. He told her he would be more than happy to, and they started back to the bungalow. They were half-way down the road when Dr. Dean stopped walking and asked,

"Mrs. Morison do you ever see lights from your house?"

Mrs. Morison hesitated.

"Why, yes, I do."

"Could you show me from where? Could you show me the place where they come from, from here?"

Mrs. Morison looked and walked to a spot in the field where she thought she saw lights from her house. Dean farm was a higher elevation than her house, and she admired the view.

"I would give anything if I could see the lights from here some night," she said.

Dr. Dean collected some stones to mark the spot from which she saw lights. They walked back to the road, and Dr. Dean's face was quite serious.

"Do you have any idea who we can report these lights to?" he asked.

"Why yes, Dr. Dean, I'm in contact with the Department of Justice."

"Really? Could I ask you to do something for me?"

"Certainly, Dr. Dean."

"Can you get a message to send me up one of the best men they have? I want the very best, not just an ordinary man who doesn't know his work."

"Dr. Dean, couldn't I do better than that? Couldn't you tell me what it is, and I will get a message to them at once? I'll telephone as soon as I get home."

"No. I don't want you to telephone, it's too dangerous. I can't tell you what I know because you're a woman, and I have no right to burden you with it."

"Why, Dr. Dean, if it is as serious as that, why haven't you sent for someone before?"

"Because I wasn't ready; two agents were here last spring, but I wasn't ready; I wanted to be perfectly sure. Now, the quicker someone comes, the better."

"I think you can trust me, Dr. Dean. If you could tell me I think I could give the message sooner."

"No, no, it's too dangerous for a woman. Would you go to Boston for me, and ask them to send a man? A good man?"

"You want me to go to Boston?"

"I know I'm asking a great deal, and I wouldn't do it unless I thought it was that important."

"If you think it's necessary, then, I'll certainly go."

"Good, good," he said.

Dr. Dean started walking again down the road, then, he stopped.

"What do you know about the Colfelts?" he asked.

"Why I don't know anything about them," Mrs. Morison answered, "I think you would know more than anyone else as they are living on your place."

"I did Mrs. Morison. I knew just a little too much. I gave them twenty-four hours to get out."

"What do you mean, Dr. Dean? What was the matter?"

Dr. Dean looked away and didn't answer. Then, he said,

"Well, I needed the rent very much, but I'm too good an American to keep people of that kind on my place."

They began walking again and he asked,

"How late can I reach you on the telephone tonight?"

"You can get me at any time as I have five telephones in my house and one right by my bed. I'm always up late, and you can reach me at any time. You needn't hesitate to call me."

"If I come out here tonight and see the lights, I'll call you up."

"Why, Dr. Dean, would that be safe?"

"I can call you up because we might talk about the turkeys even if it is late. I might say something about bringing the turkeys over, and you would know what that meant. Then if you will look out, and see what you see from your place, we can compare notes afterwards."

They walked back to the bungalow, and Mrs. Morison rejoined the other ladies who were eager to leave.

Later that night at about eleven-thirty, Mrs. Morison went up to her bedroom. Her husband was in Washington on Army business. She sat at a desk looking out onto Old

Jaffrey Road which connected Peterborough to Jaffrey and went by Dean farm. She wrote letters and was distracted by a noise in the distance. As it got closer, she recognized the sound of a high-powered automobile going by her house at a high-rate of speed. She thought there was an emergency of some sort because it was rare for an automobile to be out this late. She went back to her task, and about an hour later, was surprised again by the high whine of a car engine coming back down the road from the direction of the Dean farm. She looked out the window to see if she could recognize the vehicle, but its headlights were turned off, and it was going so fast, she couldn't make anything out.

"My, that auto is going awfully fast," she thought.

Lawrence Colfelt was in Portsmouth that night, and it took two and a half hours to drive from Portsmouth to Jaffrey. Valkenburgh and Weiss checked with the manager of the Rockingham Hotel, and he couldn't say for sure that Colfelt had been there that night. Daniel La Rose reported seeing Charles Rich driving a car on Main Street at the same time this car was going by the Morison's. Colfelt told the agents his car was in the shop in Nashua, but Valkenburgh made the observation,

"What? A guy with his money couldn't rent a vehicle?"

Chapter Eight

Charles Rich said he was kicked by his horse. The Riches had peas that night for dinner, and Mrs. Rich asked Charles to take the pods and feed them to the horse. The horse kicked out and drove the pipe he was smoking into his eye. Dr. Dean was buried on Saturday; the 17th, with no autopsy, and a rumor going around the village originating from the Rich household that Mrs. Dean killed her husband in a jealous rage. Charles Rich did not attend the funeral.

Mrs. Dean was being looked after in the bungalow by

two nurses, Mrs. Bryant and Miss Hiller. The Monday following the burial, the selectmen told the nurses that Mrs. Dean was to be moved to a sanitarium in Worcester, Mass. It was costing the town too much money for police protection and nursing help to keep her in the bungalow. Mrs. Bryant wasn't fooled. She thought it would be much easier to promote Mrs. Dean as a suspect if she weren't around to defend herself or be available for others to see she wasn't capable physically or emotionally of committing the crime. She told Valkenburgh and Weiss:

"This talk that Mrs. Dean killed her husband is absolute foolishness. She is incapable of that kind of violence, but there is talk from the Rich household about her killing her husband, and the Riches and the Deans were such good friends for so many years that I marvel at what people can say about each other. Mrs. Rich warned me about Mrs. Dean – not to be alone with her – as she might be the murderess. We moved Mrs. Dean to the hospital in Worcester yesterday, and I must say plainly, I'm ashamed of my part in this. Mr. Coolidge told me and Miss Hiller to help Dr. Childs. Mr. Coolidge said it was costing the town money for police and nurses, and they wanted to see if she was insane or not. She's no more insane than I am. She's forgetful and absentminded, yes, but insane? Not on your life. Somebody wants her out of the way so they can say what they want about her. She is a kind and gentle woman, and what people say about her, especially people who profess to be her friends, will make your blood run cold. Dr. Childs was in charge, and he told me to have Miss Hiller help me because we were forcing Mrs. Dean to do something against her will, and she could be difficult. I tried to make it as easy as I could; I tried to coax her. I kind of suggested to Mrs. Dean if she would like to take an automobile ride with us. She wanted no part of that so when it became obvious we were going to have to be forceful, Dr. Childs gave Miss Hiller a hypodermic needle with a sedative, and she snuck up behind her, and injected Mrs. Dean. Very shortly, Mrs. Dean began to get drowsy. Her face flushed which worried me, and she said,

'What if I died now? You wouldn't need to come over anymore. You have been awfully good to come here every night to stay with me.'

We helped Mrs. Dean out to the auto, and got her in the back seat – Miss Hiller on one side, and me on the other. Mr. Dillon drove. Dr. Childs followed us to Jaffrey where he left off, and we drove onto Massachusetts. Mrs. Dean would nod off and wake again and complain about being tired. She kept asking if we were taking her back to her farm, and I lied to her, and told her we were taking a roundabout way. I feel terribly about this. I'm ashamed of myself for deceiving a vulnerable, trusting woman like that. I would feel the same way lying to a child. She was getting more and more agitated about not being at home then something funny happened. I started to hum, and she said,

'I didn't know you could sing,' and she calmed right down. It was funny how my humming calmed her down even more than the sedative. When we arrived at the asylum in Worcester, she got out of the auto, and wanted to know what time it was, and I told her it was half-past three, and she said,

'We have been going for a long time. I am going to rest awhile, and then, we will start home again.'

Mrs. Dean had no idea what was going on. We got her in a chair in the waiting room, and when she closed her eyes, the three of us got out of there as fast as we could. I felt so bad; I felt like crying. We played an awfully dirty trick on that woman, and the poor dear had just lost her husband. The selectmen tried to tell me it was for the best, but I didn't feel good about it when we did it, and I don't feel any better talking to you right now. I realized after she could have stayed with me in Jaffrey, but of course, I always think of the better plan when it's too late."

Chapter Nine

From The Department of Justice report of September 16, 1918.

Colfelt is well acquainted with Charles Rich, cashier of The National Bank of Jaffrey whom he has entertained sometimes at his house. Rich was the last man to see Dean alive. Mr. Dean returned to his farm about 10:30 P.M. on August 13. The morning after the murder, August 14, Rich appeared with a black eye, and a bruise over his ear which to some he explained was caused by a kick from a horse. Immediately after the murder, Mr. Rich stated that it must have been Mrs. Dean who committed the murder, and he made that statement many times to different people.

Susan and Russell Henchman lived with their mother in a small house on Old Peterborough Road. Susan was in her early thirties, somewhat plump, with a pleasing smile. Russell was somewhat older, stocky, and a weakly-witted plumber. Susan worked at the bank with Mr. Rich, and they had a relationship. Susan was thirty years younger than Charles, but she wanted him to leave his wife, and marry her. Charles couldn't do that, and he knew it, but couldn't bring himself to tell Susan. He was a banker: the loss would be greater than the profit. It was during the spring and summer of 1918 that Susan realized she was being temporized with, and began to look for ways to make Charles jealous. It didn't take much for her to get Dr. Dean to pay attention to her. Russell was doing well as Superintendent of the Water Works, a position he got with the help of Rich. Perhaps Rich was trying to mollify Susan, but he helped Russell get several jobs. Russell was in Rich's debt, to be sure, so when The Peterborough Transcript ran the front page article on the murder on Thursday, the 15th, and stated blood stains were found in the barn and big house, it was Russell who went up to the farm to clean up. When asked by Valkenburgh why he went to the farm, Russell answered,

"I was turning off the water so the pipes wouldn't freeze."

"In August?" questioned Valkenburgh.

Chapter Ten

From The Department of Justice report of April 28, 1919:

Susan Henchman is the assistant cashier of the Monadnock National Bank and it is well-known that Rich and she are very intimate. You know what I mean. Rich has one bad fault. He is very sweet with the fair sex, and will go out of his way when he sees a nice face.

The Masons are a secret, fraternal organization whose highest allegiance is to each other. Because the Catholic Church believes that one of their purposes is to subvert the church, they are exclusively Protestant. The Masons of Jaffrey were made up of successful, Protestant business owners, managers, bankers, doctors, and mill owners. Delcie Bean and Merrill Symonds belonged to the Masons, and they owned a lumber mill in Rindge, NH. that they wanted to move to Jaffrey to be closer to the railway line. They found land suitable to their purpose for $125,000 dollars. The men went to Charles Rich for a loan, but because of the war, the money wasn't available. Rich told Bean and Symonds to try the larger banks in Boston and Worcester; they did, and had no luck. It was at a Masonic meeting that Rich proposed a syndicate of Masons to take out loans from the bank to finance the land deal. They did so, but still, they were $50,000 dollars short. Bean and Symonds bought the land so someone put in the shortfall. When Mulrooney, the Federal Bank Examiner, told Valkenburgh and Weiss about the loans, Valkenburgh asked,

"We don't know who put in the money?"

"It wasn't a loan from the bank so there's no record," said the examiner.

"There's not too many men I can think of who has that kind of money," observed Weiss.

"If it was Colfelt, then, that could be a reason for Rich not wanting him to be exposed as a German spy," said Valkenburgh.

Chapter Eleven

From The Department of Justice report of October 15, 1918:

Under our laws as I understand it, the medical examiner has no authority to make an autopsy unless ordered by the county attorney.

On Saturday, August 17, 1918, Dr. Dean was buried in The Conant Cemetery in Jaffrey. Charles Rich did not attend the funeral, and there was no autopsy performed on the body.

From the Department of Justice report of March 27, 1919:

Dekerlor inquired whether Agent left a lot of money in his home, before his departure for Europe. This question is rather significant that Agent's wife claims that Dekerlor broke into Agent's house during his absence...

On Friday night, August 23rd, Frederick Dean and Dr. Willie Wendt Dekerlor and their wives got off the evening train. The two couples were strikingly different: the Deans looked like they lived there while the Dekerlors looked like they were from the continent. He was short, strikingly handsome in a black suit with a monocle. She was plain looking with clothes that drew attention away from that. She was Elsa Schiaparelli who would later become an internationally known fashion designer on the Coco Chanel level with clients like Katherine Hepburn and Mae West. Her husband, Dr. Dekerlor, lived in two worlds: the physical and spiritual. He was an author, and free-lance writer for newspapers and a lecturer in this world, and a psychic and clairvoyant in the next. Frederick Dean and he worked as lecturers in New York City, and Frederick asked Dr. Dekerlor, who also boasted to be a criminal psychologist, to travel with him to Jaffrey to help solve the mystery of his brother's murder. Frederick had been to Jaffrey before, of course, and had met Charles Rich who was the man to see.

Saturday morning, Frederick Dean and Dr. Dekerlor met Charles Rich in his office at the bank, and right off, Dekerlor and Rich didn't like each other. Both men were arrogant, and they sensed it in each other. Rich told what he knew about the crime, and the two men listened patiently, and Dekerlor studied Rich's black eye and cuts. Rich talked about how the body was found, and how he was tied up, and the gashes on his forehead. Placing the monocle in his eye, Dekerlor asked,

"These gashes you speak of, how many were there?"

"Three," answered Rich.

"How would they get there?"

"A garden cultivator was found at the scene – a three-pronged garden cultivator which he was struck with."

"How long were the gash marks?"

Rich gave an impatient sigh.

"I'm not really sure about that. I was told an inch and a half."

If Dekerlor was irritating Rich before, he made it worse,

"Looks like you got quite a whack on your face?"

Rich peevishly answered how he carried pea pods in a basket out to his horse, and because of the fresh sawdust put down, startled the horse, and she kicked out, hitting the basket, and knocking the pipe he was smoking up into his eye. Rich stopped talking and Dekerlor was thinking,

"Well, how can a horse kick a man's face, and make a cut here, and a cut there, with such a large black eye? More likely a fist made that black eye than a pipe, I would wager."

Rich was irritated for two reasons. He didn't like explaining himself to an outsider, and an arrogant, pompous outsider was even worse. Rich started talking about Mrs. Dean killing her husband, and how they moved her to a sanitarium in Worcester to see if she's insane or not. That made Frederick Dean angry even though he'd had problems getting along with Mary Dean, that description of her by Rich was insulting. Rich had successfully parried with Mrs. Dean Dr. Dekerlor's thrust of how'd–you–get–your–black eye?

Frederick stood up. As they walked out of the bank, Dekerlor asked,

"Let's go have a look at the crime scene, shall we?"

The two men rented an auto, and drove up to Dean farm. Dekerlor had with him a magnifying glass and camera. Dekerlor believed photographs captured a crime scene, and if one had the gift, one could read the photograph for clues; even clues that were otherworldly. Dekerlor stood next to the auto and admired the view.

"Lovely view of the mountain," he said.

The two men walked around the farm, and stopped at the barn porch. Dekerlor carefully examined the barn porch with the magnifying glass, and then took photographs. They walked up to the well, and Dekerlor examined the well, around it, and found scratch marks in the foundation of the big house which he photographed. Smugness came over Dekerlor when he told Frederick,

"I have a hypothesis."

"Really?"

"Yes. You see, there were scratch marks on Rich's face as there are scratch marks in the barn porch and foundation of the big house, and Rich told us of the gashes on your brother's forehead, so if I can connect the scratches from all four locations, then, wouldn't that place Mr. Rich at the crime scene?"

"My brother's already been buried."

"We'll exhume him."

"I thought you could talk to the dead? Wouldn't that be easier?"

"Communing with the victim of a violent death is difficult."

"Oh?" said Frederick.

Chapter Twelve

From The Department of Justice report of September 23, 1919.

Frederick Dean said that he was so disgusted with Dekerlor that he decided to go back to New York, and not have anything more to do with the case, particularly as Pickard pressed him with the fact that probably Mrs. Dean in her deranged mind murdered her husband...

On Sunday night, a sheriff showed up at Frederick Dean's hotel door, and informed him that Roy Pickard, the county prosecutor, wanted to see him Monday night at the Keene jail.

On Monday morning, Dr. Dekerlor and Frederick Dean met with the selectmen. The selectmen didn't feel comfortable with strangers, foreign strangers' even worse and foreign strangers' who were doctors even worse than that. Frederick Dean spoke first,

"Gentlemen, thank-you for seeing us this morning. May I introduce Dr. Willie Wendt Dekerlor who's here to help me investigate my brother's murder. Dr. Dekerlor in the vice-president of the International Congress for Experimental Psychology, and the author of several books, and a correspondent for The New York World and The Boston American."

The selectmen slowly nodded their heads.

"Dr. Dekerlor has completed a preliminary examination of the murder scene, and has gathered evidence which leads us to make the following request. We ask permission to exhume my brother's body..."

"What?" Peter Hogan cried out.

Dr. Dekerlor opened his mouth to speak, but Coolidge got the attention.

"Gentlemen, gentlemen, gentlemen, before we go any further, I would like an opportunity to talk with our visitor to get to know him better. It is unusual for us to have such a distinguished visitor in our town. Good morning, Doctor."

"Good morning."

"I hope you're finding the village of Jaffrey friendly, sir?"

"Quaint might be the word."

"Yes. What is your occupation?"

"I am a psychologist – a criminal psychologist, and a doctor and lecturer."

"Very good. When you say doctor, do you mean physician?"

"Doctor of Philosophy."

"Interesting. Where are you from, sir?"

"My wife works in fashion and helps others with the occult so we reside in Paris, and have an apartment in Greenwich Village as well."

Coolidge chuckled, and the two other selectmen, after picking up on the cue, chuckled too.

"My! You must find New Hampshire boring?"

Dr. Dekerlor removed the monocle from his eye.

"Quaint, like I said, but I gave my word to my friend; I would help him uncover the circumstances of his brother's death."

"How do you know Frederick Dean?"

"We are lecturers in Manhattan. Same circuit, different topics however."

There was silence until Boynton asked,

"You speak more than one language?"

"Yes, I speak five languages. I speak German and French best of all. I speak English, Polish, and Italian next best, and Spanish afterward. I have studied about eighteen other languages besides; I can read them, but I don't speak them much. I know some Russian. I travel extensively, and am very well-known, not only in New York, Washington, and in France, as well as, England and Italy, but I am very well known probably all over the world through my various writings, and my various activities."

There was silence while the selectmen tried to grasp the magnitude of the man across from them.

"Your English is good," said Hogan.

The two other selectmen slowly turned and looked at Hogan.

"You want to exhume Dr. Dean's body?" asked Coolidge.

"Yes," answered Frederick Dean, "Dr. Dekerlor has…"

"If I may sir," interrupted Dekerlor putting his monocle in his eye.

"You see, I have measurements taken at the crime scene

which when I match them to the scratches on an individual's face will place that individual at the crime scene."

"Remarkable," said Boynton.

"But for me to be reliable, I need the marks from the victim's forehead."

The selectmen didn't like the sound of that, and there was silence until Coolidge spoke,

"Well, I would ask that we adjourn this meeting until after lunch which would allow the selectmen time to consider your sensitive request. We would have to consider the family…"

"Mrs. Dean is in Worcester," interjected Frederick Dean.

"This meeting is adjourned until one o'clock," stated Coolidge.

Feri Weiss before joining The Department of Justice was an immigration inspector in New York Harbor, and knew of the Dekerlors'. He knew their reputation for Bolshevik sympathies, and that they had been deported from England in the summer of 1915 for cheating people out of money.

Chapter Thirteen

From The Department of Justice report for June 26, 1919.

Mr. Dekerlor stated to me that he had been very closely watched by the British Secret Service the last few months, and has been followed by more Secret Service agents than ever before. Furthermore he expressed a surprise that Agent hasn't arrested him yet, and asked, "When are you going to arrest me?" When Agent asked him "why" he said, "Oh, because I am talking against England and along Bolshevik lines."

Coolidge stood at a window, and watched Frederick Dean and Dr. Dekerlor on the street below. He heard a voice in the background, and turned from the window, and realized it was Boynton talking.

"Just tell him while we respect – or maybe even admire his expertise, this is a town matter, and has to be dealt with by town authorities."

Hogan agreed, saying,

"We don't want an outsider like that poking around in our town business. Which of us has not benefitted from a favor from Charles?"

Coolidge sat at a desk, and put his head in his hands, and loudly said,

"You're overlooking something."

The two selectmen looked at Coolidge.

"What?" said Hogan.

Coolidge dropped his hands and looked up.

"The man writes for two major newspapers. He could make us the laughingstock of the country."

No one spoke until Coolidge said,

"No gentlemen, I think we let him have his way."

"But Bill, he's going to make trouble for Charles," said Boynton, "We all know Charles can rub people the wrong way especially people that don't know him."

"I agree, Ed, but there's nothing we can do about that. This exhuming of the body is a crack-pot idea, and if we make a stipulation we have to be present to observe his findings, then, all we have to do is claim that his findings were inconclusive, and this whole trick will go nowhere."

"But what if he is conclusive?" taunted Hogan.

"You're going to prove murder with scratch marks?" answered Boynton.

"Remember this man is world renowned."

"So what's he doing in Jaffrey?" argued Boynton.

"Putting one over on the country-bumpkins," answered Coolidge.

The sheriff made it plain to Frederick Dean that his meeting with the county solicitor was private. Frederick tried talking Dr. Dekerlor out of coming to Keene with him, but the moment Dekerlor smelled intrigue he was not to be denied. Monday night, the two men had dinner at a restaurant, and went to the Keene Jail to meet Roy Pickard. The sheriffs detained Dekerlor in a holding area while Frederick went into the jailer's office. Roy Pickard and Sheriff Lord were there, and they introduced themselves to Frederick.

"This man you're traveling with, how well do you know him?" asked Pickard.

Fredrick Dean squirmed in his chair.

"I know him from the lecture circuit in New York. I see he's eccentric, but he's also highly charismatic which most people misunderstand."

Pickard studied Frederick, and then said,

"Do you know he's being followed by the British Secret Service for possible ties to the Bolshevik Party?"

"No, I didn't know that."

"It's not my decision, but I would caution you; your association with him is more dangerous than you think."

"I see."

"Besides the investigation is focused on Mary Dean who we believe killed her husband in a jealous rage."

"Well, sir, I don't know about that. Mary never liked me, and the feeling was mutual, but even with that, I have a hard time believing she could do something like that."

"I understand your sentiments, Mr. Dean, but you don't know how much her mind may have deteriorated from the last time you saw her."

"That's true."

"But the more pressing problem is your association with Dr. Dekerlor, and I want to ask you if you would consider going back to New York, and taking him with you? You can see we've got enough problems around here as it is, and the last thing we need is a flamboyant character in the middle of it, trying to make a name for himself."

"I don't know as I have much influence over Dr. Dekerlor. I will try, if that's what you think is best, but I don't hold out any promises."

"I understand," said Pickard.

Dr. Dekerlor would not have been good at what he was if he weren't acutely aware of others' feelings. On the auto ride back to Jaffrey, he sensed a change in his friend, Frederick Dean, and was wily enough to be patient to see what was revealed. It was the following morning, after a visit to Charles Rich, that things became apparent. The men walked out of the bank, and Dekerlor asked,

"Did you see the cuts on his face were healed?"

"He never had cuts on his face," answered Frederick.

Dekerlor abruptly stopped.

"What Mr. Dean? We've spoken all the time about the cuts on Rich's face. Now you want to deny it? Do you, Mr. Dean, resort to lying?"

"You're a fine one to accuse me of lying."

"I thought you wanted justice for your brother's murder, and here, you let some small-town lawyer talk you out of it."

"These people don't want us here, Dr. Dekerlor. I'm telling you, Dr. Dekerlor, they don't want us here. I'm going back to New York, and you should come with me. You should leave with me."

The men started walking.

"I'm afraid that's not possible, Mr. Dean. I don't run away from difficulties. I'm sorry that Lawyer Pickard has conned you out of what you really want."

That afternoon, before getting on the train, Fredrick tried once again to get Dekerlor to get on the train with him, but got on the train alone.

About a week later, an ad appeared in The Peterborough Transcript:

"World Renowned Clairvoyant & Palmist, Dr. Willie Wendt Dekerlor is available for tea readings at the Granite State Hotel, Room 302, from three to five, Wednesday afternoons. Fees Negotiated. The Future Is In Your Palms."

Chapter Fourteen

Two married women: Adele Johnson and Edith Foster came to the door and knocked. Edith slipped her wedding band off her finger. The door opened, and there stood, the short, but handsome, Dr. Dekerlor in his black suit. He slightly bowed and motioned the women in. The shades were drawn, and the room was lit by candles. There was a table in the middle of the room with a crystal ball.

"How can I be of assistance this afternoon, ladies?" purred Dekerlor. The women smelled incense. Dekerlor pointed to a chair at the table, and brought another for the second woman. Dekerlor placed the monocle in his eye, and studied the two women.

"I would like my palm read, and maybe some clairvoyance after," said Adele.

"Hummmm…yes, I see," said the doctor, "clairvoyance is for the living and the future, and a medium is to commune with the dead and past."

"I want to talk with Martha Washington," blurted out Edith.

Dekerlor chuckled.

"I'm afraid it doesn't work that way. You see, you must

have some corporal connection to the person you're communing with."

"Oh!" exclaimed Edith.

"I would like you to predict my future," asked Adele.

"All right, then – let's close your eyes and concentrate. Your hand, please."

Adele hesitated, and then, gave her hand. Edith giggled.

"Shhh!" hissed the doctor.

Edith blushed. Dekerlor moved his thumbs over Adele's palm while looking at the ceiling.

"I see three children," he said

"That ain't right!" exclaimed Edith.

"Two. A boy and girl."

"I'm sorry that's not right either," said Adele.

Edith giggled.

"Quiet please! You're interfering with my concentration."

Dekerlor refocused his concentration.

"I see one child," he said.

"Brilliant!" exclaimed Edith.

"There's negative energy in the room that is interfering with my ability to read accurately," complained the doctor.

"Bet there's no interference when it comes time to pay the bill," observed Edith.

"Your child is a boy," said Dekerlor.

"Wrong again," pointed out Edith.

"I see the number forty-five," said Dekerlor.

"I don't know what that is," said Adele.

"Your age perhaps?"

"Wrong again!" snapped Edith, "You charge people money for this?"

Dekerlor gave Edith a dirty look.

"There's too much negative energy in the room."

"Try me then," suggested Edith extending her hand, palm up.

"Of course, Mademoiselle."

"Ha!" exclaimed Edith as she pulled her wedding ring from her pocket.

Feri Weiss talked to Walter Lindsay who was a part-time police officer in Jaffrey. Walter said,

"There was a story in town about how Dr. Dean evicted the Colfelts from his farm, and nobody knew for sure why it happened, but people didn't much care for Colfelt so nobody was too upset. On July 13, a month after the Colfelts left, I met Dr. Dean in front of the post office. He noticed my police badge, and asked me if I were on the force. I told him yes. Then, he said, 'I have lived on the farm for twenty-eight years, and I have never been molested in any way, shape, or manner, but if I wanted police protection, where would I telephone to?' I told him either the station, Duncan's or Fred Stratton's livery stable."

Chapter Fifteen

From The Department of Justice report of April, 17, 1919.

Upon Agent's question as to what the probable basis for their alleged prejudice was, Colfelt replied that it was because he had nothing in common with the villagers, and did not mix with them; that they therefore did not understand him, and became antagonistic and proceeded to gossip irresponsibly about him.

Roy Pickard was not an elected County Attorney. Pickard was appointed by Judge John Kivel to the position after the man who was elected stepped down. It was a reward for being a loyal party member. Charles Rich spent time in the House and Senate, and when Charles Rich said Mrs. Dean killed her husband; Roy Pickard said Mrs. Dean killed her husband. Pickard proclaimed he found evidence of Mrs. Dean's involvement when he discovered a tortoise shell hairpin near the well. Valkenburgh and Weiss had misgivings about Pickard when he didn't order an autopsy on the body, and the hasty removal of Mrs. Dean from her home. When the Colfelts were traveling, Feri Weiss talked to Mr. Ash of Temple who was the caretaker of the house the Colfelts were renting, and he agreed to let Feri into the house. In the second floor bathroom, Feri found a tortoise shell hairpin, and when Valkenburgh visited Mrs. Dean in Worcester, while she was distracted by a nurse, he surreptitiously removed a hairpin which was not tortoise shell.

It was the end of August when the men gathered at the headstone which read: William K. Dean, 1855-1918. The selectmen were there: William Coolidge, Peter Hogan, and Edward Boynton; and the undertaker, Mr. Leighton; and Dr. Dekerlor; Reverend Enslin; and two doctors, Childs and Dinsmoor; Charles Rich; and Charlie Nute, Chief of Police. Mr. Johnson who owned the photography shop in Jaffrey was there to take pictures. He was setting up his tripod and camera. The casket was out of the ground, and Mr. Leighton was wiping off the dirt. Mr. Coolidge stepped forward, and said,

"Gentlemen, may we bow our heads?"

The men removed hats and bowed their heads while Reverend Enslin said a prayer. After Amen was said, the men stirred. Mr. Leighton went to the coffin, and loosened the top with a hammer and pry bar. When the corpse was revealed, several men stepped back. The rest of the men moved out of the way so Mr. Johnson could take photographs. He took a photo, and moved the tripod, adjusted the angle of the camera, and took another photo, and repeated it again. Then it was the Doctors' turn to examine the body. Dr. Dekerlor watched with a paper in his hand. The doctors noted the gashes on the forehead. When they finished, Dr. Dekerlor came to the casket. He closely looked at the forehead before placing the paper over the gashes. He traced the gashes marks onto the paper. He straightened up and said,

"Gentlemen, if you would be so kind to meet me at Dean farm."

About a half and hour later, the group of men gathered near the barn porch. Dekerlor spoke,

"Gentlemen, I've found scratch marks in three locations that if I can match to a fourth location will place that individual at the scene of the murder. Marked on my paper – which you observed me do – are the scratch marks from the victim's forehead."

Dekerlor bent over and lined up the scratch marks on the paper to the scratch marks in the barn porch. Several of the men moved closer. When he was satisfied the men saw what he wanted them to see, he walked up to the big house, and when the men gathered, he said,

"The third set of scratch marks is here on the foundation."

Again when he was satisfied the men saw what he wanted them to see, he walked up to Charles Rich, and placed the paper up against Rich's face, and said,

"Strange to relate, these marks on the paper fit the marks on Rich's face. Mr. Rich tell us, where did you get your black eye?"

"At the right time and place, I will tell," answered Rich.

Rich told investigators he was kicked right before nine, and there was one man who knew that wasn't true. Albany Pelletier was a French-Canadian night watchman at Bean and Symonds the night of the murder, and he saw Ed Baldwin and Rich's horse and buggy at the saw-dust chute when he made his nine o'clock rounds. As a French-Canadian workingman there wasn't too many people who'd listen to what he had to say. One night late, he walked to the rectory. A single window was lit in the rectory. He knocked on the door and waited. He was about to knock for the second time, when the door swung open, and a woman holding a candle stood there.

"Is Father Hennon available?" he asked.

"One moment."

The light receded down the hallway, and after several moments, came back again.

"Come in," she said.

He entered the door, and followed the woman down the hallway. She knocked on a door before opening it, and guided him into a room where Father Hennon was reading. She left the room, closing the door behind her, and Father Hennon took off his glasses. He was a handsome man with a thick crop of black hair and a well-proportioned face.

"Albany," he said, "this is unexpected."

"I know Father, and I'm sorry to disturb you like this. There is something weighing on me, and I don't want another restless night. I hate to disturb you at this late hour, but I know I won't be able to sleep until I can share this with someone."

"I see," said the priest motioning Albany to a chair. "You couldn't share this burden with your wife?"

"I have, Father, but I need to tell someone in authority."

Father Hennon smiled.

"Albany, I don't know how much corporeal authority I have."

"I need some guidance as to what to do," Albany earnestly said.

"I see. Tell me what's troubling you, and we'll see if I can help."

There was the rumble of thunder in the distance.

"Father, the night of the murder, I saw Charles Rich's horse and buggy at the sawdust chute at nine o'clock."

The two men made eye contact.

"I don't think I understand," said the priest.

Albany leaned forward in his chair.

"Rich is telling everyone he was kicked in his barn right before nine; he swears to it. How can it be if I saw what I saw?"

The men heard a clap of thunder.

"Oh yes, yes, indeed, I see your problem. You saw Charles Rich at the sawdust chute?"

"No, no, Father, it was Ed Baldwin, but it was Rich's horse and buggy. That I know for sure."

"Why would Ed Baldwin be driving Rich's horse and buggy?"

"They share a barn, and sometimes Baldwin comes to the chute for bags of sawdust."

"With Rich's horse and buggy?"

"Yes, Father."

"You're certain of this?"

"Yes, Father, I am."

There was a loud clap of thunder. In the silence after, Albany asked,

"What should I do, Father?"

The priest stood up and walked to a window, and looked out for several moments, before he said,

"Albany is difficult as this is, I'm glad your shared your burden with me. The authorities should be notified of what you saw. What were you doing at Bean and Symonds at nine in the evening?"

"I was the night watchman that night, and I was making my nine o'clock rounds, and that's when I saw Ed Baldwin at the chute. I was fired a week after when I told my supervisor about what I'd seen; he claimed I was sleeping on the job which wasn't true."

"No wonder you can't sleep."

"Rich has a lot of influence in this town, and I know if I say anything, it will bring me trouble."

"You're doing the right thing, Albany, and the problem now is who do we talk to so we won't be ignored? I think our best chances are with the Federal men."

"You cross those town guys and it makes it hard to get a job," said Albany.

"I understand Albany."

There was the peal of thunder.

"Sounds like I'm going to get wet," joked Albany.

Chapter Sixteen

Charles Rich and his friends were angry at the accusation made by Dr. Dekerlor. Roy Pickard after initial cooperation with Dekerlor withdrew support which created animosity between the men. The Masons saw Dekerlor as a grandstanding, self-aggrandizing promoter who was exploiting the tragedy for his own purposes. Dekerlor did have a flair for the theatrical as when he announced he had important, new evidence to show, and a group of farmers, shop clerks, and a newspaper reporter gathered in the lobby of The Granite State Hotel to see what he had. He'd gotten the keys from the selectmen, and had gone through the buildings on the farm, and found some postcards in Natalye Colfelt's bedroom which he thought were significant. He started this way:

"Gentlemen, I have been investigating the buildings on Dean farm, and am pleased to announce, I have found important, new evidence that I feel will explain why Dr. Dean was murdered."

He held a cardboard box in the air.

"Inside this cardboard box which I found in the former residence of the Colfelts contains fifty or so postcards made up from photographs taken by Colfelt's daughter for her college friends. Seemingly innocent postcards until you examine them more closely. All fifty postcards contain the same objects, but it is the order of how the objects are arranged that becomes significant."

Dr. Dekerlor set the box on a table, and held up a single postcard.

"This postcard, which can be made up at any photographer's shop, was made up from a photo negative of Colfelt's daughter. In this postcard, you will see various, and apparently, random objects on a mantelpiece. You will please observe the objects on the mantelpiece are a toy dog, a stuffed teddy bear, a child doll, and a clock. A seemingly innocent postcard, Gentlemen, until you begin to go through all fifty or so of the postcards, and it is then, you will observe the significance of the postcards." He took his monocle from his eye, and spun it, flashing light around the room.

"What you will observe upon further examination is that the order or sequence of the objects on the mantelpiece changes every eighth postcard or so, and I submit to you, Gentlemen, that this is a code used by the Germans to communicate intelligence."

The men murmured.

"At every eighth postcard in this box, the order of the objects on the mantelpiece changes, and the position of the hands on the clock change in each postcard, and I say to you, Gentlemen, that the objects on the mantelpiece represent constellations in the northern sky, and the hands on the clock tell the time the signals are to be sent. Each object on the mantelpiece represents a constellation. The toy dog represents the constellation, Canis Major, and the stuffed teddy bear represents the constellation, Ursa Major, and the child doll represents the constellation, Perseus."

Dekerlor replace his monocle.

"I am European, and know how clever the Germans are with astronomy, and when I discovered these postcards, in the former residence of the Colfelts, I saw through their ruse, and interpreted them as a code of some kind. Further examination of my theory reveals these three constellations form a triangle in the northern sky. These three constellations form a forty-five degree triangle in the sky which the Germans use to communicate their messages. If you examine it, you see the bear constellation is on the left, the child constellation is at the apex, and the dog constellation is on the right. There's your forty-five degree triangle. Now, those three constellations are the positions in the sky where the lights are to be flashed which gives the message, and the hands on the clock give the time the messages are to be sent."

Dekerlor paused to give his audience a moment to assimilate his brilliance.

"Now, if the first signal light is at the apex of the triangle or the child and the second signal light goes to the right or the dog, and the third goes to the left, the bear, that would be one message. The direction of the light goes from right to left. To change the direction of the signal lights in the sky, the spies change the order of the objects on the mantelpiece in the postcard. Like I said, the order of the objects in the postcard changes every eighth postcard to change the direction of the signals in the sky. If the child is first, then the bear, and finally the dog, the lights go from left to right, and then back to the child. They're using the same forty-five degree triangle, but the direction the signal light travels changes the message."

A big farmer asked,

"What you're telling us is if the first signal is at the apex of this triangle you're talking about, and the second signal is to the right, and the final one is to the left, the message would be – let's say, Boston, right?"

"Yes," answered Dekerlor.

"All right then. If the first signal is at the apex, and the second signal is to the left, and the last signal is to the right, the message would be different, something like, say, Portsmouth?"

"Exactly," said Dekerlor, "the Germans use the same triangle, and change the message by going either left to right or right to left. They could even use multiple flashes in the three positions to have more messages."

The man holding a notebook, and pencil asked,

"The signals are flashed from Monadnock?"

"I've been told there's a cave near the summit which would suit their purpose."

The man wrote what Dekerlor said, and then, asked,

"Do you think this guy – the tenant on Dean farm, Coldfield, was signaling, and Dean was onto him?"

"These postcards prove that."

"Some people are angry with you for accusing Rich," said the man with the notebook.

"Mr. Rich is a banker, and Colfelt has money from somewhere so the idea they maybe confederates is not out of the question."

"You think both men killed Dean?"

"Why does that surprise you? Good day, Gentlemen," said Dekerlor.

Chapter Seventeen

There was a long pause when Father Hennon told Valkenburgh and Weiss about what he learned about Rich's horse.

"One of your parishioners told you he saw Rich's horse at Bean and Symonds at nine the night of the murder?" he repeated to grasp the significance of what he heard.

"Yes," quietly answered the priest.

"Father, you know we have to confirm this for ourselves," said Weiss.

"Yes, I was fearful of that."

"You believe what you were told?" asked Valkenburgh.

"Certainly. I've know the man for several years, and he is incapable of deceit."

"You understand we have to talk to him."

The priest handed Valkenburgh a piece of paper.

"Thank-you," said Valkenburgh.

Norman Gifford was the assistant superintendent of the Boston office of The Department of Justice. A bald man in his mid-forties, who never married, he started out as a street cop in New York. He'd learned there are vile people in the world, and the only way to be successful was to be smarter than they were. In most cases that wasn't difficult. He sent a telegraph to Valkenburgh in New Hampshire: Return to Boston, Post Haste. NG

The three men sat in Gifford's office with the window half-way opened and a breeze that ruffled papers on his desk. Gifford sat behind the big desk, and Valkenburgh and Weiss sat in chairs. Weiss read a newspaper. Gifford was reading reports and Valkenburgh looked out the window.

"Ruth's having a good year," murmured Weiss.

"It was smart to move him," distractedly agreed Gifford. There was the sound of a truck on the street below.

"Okay!" exclaimed Gifford as he put down the report, "tell me what's going on in New Hampshire?"

Valkenburgh and Weiss recognized the cue and focused on Gifford.

"I'm not sure we know exactly," admitted Valkenburgh.

"From what I'm reading in your reports there seems to be some funny stuff going on. Do you have any leads on the lights?"

"We get reports from women mostly that seem overblown. They see colored rockets and balloons, and space ships, for Christ Sakes," said Valkenburgh.

"Not always though," interjected Weiss, "there's some that seem reasonable."

"But you don't have any solid leads or do you?" asked Gifford.

"Dean was murdered," proposed Valkenburgh.

"Because of the lights?"

Valkenburgh and Weiss looked at each other.

"We can't say that definitely, no," said Weiss.

"Who was the chap with the black eye…?"

"Charles Rich, a banker, and good friend of Dean's who showed up when the body was found with a black eye."

Gifford looked up at the ceiling.

"Hummm," he hummed.

"In New Hampshire, the County Prosecutor has to order an autopsy from the County Medical Examiner, and in this case, Roy Pickard didn't do that…" explained Weiss.

"Who's Roy Pickard?"

"The county attorney…"

"I think we can agree that not ordering an autopsy in an unsolved homicide is an odd choice. Why would they do that?"

"Charles Rich and Roy Pickard are pushing hard Mrs. Dean as the suspect in her husband's killing. They've got her in a sanitarium in Worcester."

"So they didn't autopsy the body because of the evidence that might make Mrs. Dean less of a suspect?"

Valkenburgh and Weiss looked at each other.

"I wouldn't say no to that," said Valkenburgh.

"It's a small farming town, and there's a group of men who are very tight, and who pull the strings so to speak, and that's why it's as murky as it is. Roy Pickard is taking orders…" said Weiss.

"Well, I don't take orders so I'm going to hire Doctor McGrath to do an autopsy on the body, and we'll see what that brings us. Now wasn't there some business about the horse?"

"The Catholic priest told us that one of his parishioners who was the watchman at Bean and Symonds saw Rich's horse at the sawdust chute at the time he was being kicked in his barn…" explained Weiss.

Gifford tapped his fingers together.

"I see," he said.

"A French Catholic workingman would be ignored by Protestants. That's why the priest is talking to us."

"I would stay on that unless you discover something that disqualifies it. I think we have to do something unexpected to see if we can catch them off-guard. Sometimes if you do the unexpected, the subject will cough up something they didn't want to."

"I don't know. Small towns are tough to crack," observed Valkenburgh.

"Surprise somebody who doesn't expect it, but you think would have information you want is the idea. And be tough in the interview to scare them if you can."

"You mean a supporting player so to speak?" asked Weiss.

"Georgiana Hodgkins," said Valkenburgh.

"Perfect!" exclaimed Weiss.

"Who's Georgiana Hodgkins?"

"Charles Rich's sister-in-law who was at his house the night of the murder."

"Perfect!" exclaimed Gifford.

Chapter Eighteen

From The Department of Justice report of August 10, 1918.

A great many of these reports on the lights have come from women who are intimately acquainted with one another, and it appears to have become a hobby with them to report these occurrences. During interviews which agent has had with them, they constantly refer to one another relative to what has been seen. Apparently no one living in the immediate vicinity from which these lights are alleged to have been displayed has seen them.

The state election for Governor took place on the fifth, and on the eleventh, the war was over. John Bartlett, a Republican and a Mason, won the governorship, and he appointed as his attorney general, Oscar Young, also a Mason.

Georgiana Hodgkins lived with her mother on Long Island, and taught English at the Washington Irving High School in Manhattan. She visited her sister and brother-in-law on weekends and holidays. Lana Rich understood how taxing their mother was, and felt sorry for her sister. Valkenburgh and Weiss took the train from Boston to New York, and went to the Washington Irving High School. The Principal was surprised at why they were there, and even more so, by whom they wanted to talk. He led the men to an empty classroom, and several minutes later, there was a knock on the door. Georgiana came in, her face pale, and her eyes darting around the room.

"Please, have a seat," offered Valkenburgh.

She sat at a student desk not looking at either man.

"I'm Agent Valkenburgh and this is Agent Weiss from The Department of Justice, and I assume you know why we're here."

Georgiana coughed, and took a beat to compose herself.

"Yes," she whispered.

Valkenburgh asked her to tell them how her brother-in-law got his black eye. Between her coughing and whispering voice, Valkenburgh, several times, had to ask her to repeat herself. There had been several indications over the summer that Rich and Dr. Dean weren't getting along, and so Rich's version of Dr. Dean visiting his house the night of the murder was important to Rich as proof there was no falling out between the two men even though there were sightings of Dr. Dean on his way home earlier than what Rich reported, never mind, that Mrs. Dean said her husband was back at the farm at nine-thirty. Valkenburgh asked,

"Are you positive that Mr. Rich had a black eye, and bruised face, at the time Dr. Dean left?"

"Yes."

"What did Mr. Rich say as to how he got his black eye?"

"He said he went in the barn, where the horse was eating, and he put his hand on her, and she kicked out, and hit Mr. Rich in the face, and knocked his pipe in his face."

Weiss asked,

"What time did this happen?"

"Right around nine o'clock."

"What was he carrying?"

"I don't know."

She had a spasm of coughing, and Valkenburgh offered her a handkerchief which she declined. Valkenburgh asked her,

"Did you talk it over with Mr. and Mrs. Rich in reference as to what to say when anyone would ask you?"

"Positively no."

"Your answers are the same as Mrs. Rich's," accused Weiss.

"That's because we have been talking about it between us which is only natural."

Valkenburgh asked,

"How did Mr. Rich hear of the murder of Dean?"

"Some rumor from the village."

"Are you sure Mr. and Mrs. Rich didn't receive word over the telephone?"

"I'm sure they didn't receive word over the telephone."

"Then the records in the telephone office calling Rich's house from Dean's house are wrong?"

Georgiana had a fit of coughing. She said,

"I wish I could talk more, but I have such a very bad cold. I hope Mr. Rich won't be mixed up in this – for you know – circumstantial evidence is very bad. Mr. Rich appeared the next day with a black eye. You know Dr. Dean saw the black eye when he was at Mr. Rich's house, but he is dead, and there is no one else except the family to prove he had a black eye."

"That is a problem, isn't it?" commented Weiss "especially since Mrs. Dean testified her husband was back on the farm when Rich said he was at Rich's house."

"And she was the last to see him alive…"

"Presuming no one came onto the farm," said Valkenburgh.

Georgiana coughed so badly she excused herself.

Chapter Nineteen

January of 1919 a Masonic Governor and Attorney General took office in Concord, and on a bitterly cold day, Dr. George Magrath traveled to Jaffrey to perform an autopsy on the five month interred body of Dr. Dean. It took soldiers from Fort Devens working with pick axes to get the coffin out of the cement-like ground which they carried into a receiving tomb. At two in the afternoon, Valkenburgh and Weiss, the selectmen, and Mr. Leighton, the undertaker arrived at the receiving tomb to watch Dr. Magrath perform an autopsy. One of the selectman brought a small oil heater to off-set the cold. Dr. Magrath handed out oil-scented handkerchiefs to the spectators which they quickly used when the top of the coffin came off, and a stench filled the tomb. Valkenburgh and Weiss helped Dr. Magrath lift the partially decomposed body of Dr. Dean out of the coffin, and lay it on a wooden platform. Dr. Magrath removed the coat and shirt. He went over the body. He took out a saw to cut open the skull, and held Dr. Dean's head like a football. When he began to saw, the head slipped from his grasp. Feri Weiss took the head in his hands and held it while Dr. Magrath sawed. As the doctor sawed, body fluid splashed up onto Weiss's face. Valkenburgh took out his handkerchief, and wiped Weiss's face. When Dr. Magrath had an incision, he stuck his finger in. Magrath said he wanted to turn the body over which Weiss helped him do. After he was finished, the two agents helped him return the body to the coffin.

Dr. Magrath found that the victim's skull was fractured, and his neck broken, and there was a new understanding that the attack was more violent than thought. Valkenburgh was curious as to what the doctors treating Mrs. Dean thought of the autopsy findings so he and Weiss took the train to Worcester. They met the head of the hospital, and told him of the autopsy finding.

"Doesn't surprise me," said the doctor.

"That's what we thought too," said Weiss.

"Mrs. Dean is not capable of that kind of violence, neither physically or temperamentally. I have spent much time observing and evaluating Mrs. Dean, and it is a total physical impossibility for her to have murdered her husband the way he was murdered."

"More like two men, I should think," suggested Valkenburgh.

"Yes, that makes more sense," agreed the doctor.

"Who was the second man?" asked Weiss.

"Thank-you, Doctor," said Valkenburgh standing.

Roy Pickard and Dr. Dekerlor didn't like each other much: the lawyer thought the doctor a charlatan, and the doctor thought the attorney incompetent. Neither man was happy when they ended up at the January meeting of the Grange in Jaffrey. Both were asked to give an appraisal of where the murder investigation was, and Roy Pickard spoke first. He said Mrs. Dean was the suspect, and furthermore there had not been enough evidence collected to justify a Grand Jury Hearing which was being proposed by Father Hennon. Speaking first gave Pickard the chance to cross-examine Dekerlor when he spoke.

"Gentlemen," began the doctor, "it is my pleasure to report to you the most startling discovery that I made from taking photographs of the crime scene. I took photographs of the barn porch where Dr. Dean was attacked, and blood stains were found. Later on, when I was developing the negatives, there was nothing out of the ordinary, until I saw a small, whitish formation on the negative. I looked at it more closely, and amazingly saw a man's face. There was no mistaking it: I recognized the face. When I looked further, three other faces appeared, one of them a woman's"

A murmur went through the audience at the extraordinariness of this information punctuated by Pickard's voice,

"Can you show us the photograph? I'm certain we're all most curious to see the photograph."

"I'm afraid not. It's with a psychic colleague in Boston."

"Of course, of course, making an exorbitant claim with no evidence!" exclaimed Pickard.

"I didn't know I would be asked to speak tonight," snapped back the doctor.

"It is against my better judgment, but I'll ask the question regardless, who was the face you saw in the negative?"

"Charles Rich."

"Just as I thought. And that was the only face you recognized?"

"There was another face, but it revealed itself only to one who has extrasensory powers."

"Would you be willing to share that information with those of us who aren't as gifted?"

"The lawyer, Mr. Smith."

"Reginald Smith of Boston?"

"Yes, that's correct."

Pickard turned to the audience.

"How can that be? Reginald Smith didn't know anything about the murder until after it happened."

"Your ignorance is that you don't comprehend metaphysics. This is something that is known only to a very few. I would suggest there are various categories of thinkers – there are thinkers who are within the bounds of the philosophical, and others who go into metaphysics, and others still who are, perhaps, more advanced than either, whom besides having a metaphysical understanding have a metaphysical vision."

"Metaphysical vision? Metaphysical vision?" boomed Pickard, "Who in God's Name knows what metaphysical vision is?" Pickard paused and stared at the audience to give greater affect to his question.

"I don't quite understand you sir," he continued, "Let me see if I can make this more understandable to those of us who don't have metaphysical vision. The reason why Charles Rich's face appeared in the negative was because he was there when the blood stains which were part of the negative were made. Have I got that right?"

"Yes, that's correct."

"So how is it that Lawyer Smith's face would be in the negative when he didn't even learn about the murder until a considerable time after it happened? He wasn't there when the photograph was taken."

"Those of us in the occult know this to be a prophetic picture, a prophetic projection of the event."

Pickard paced back and forth.

"You mean to say the negative that was developed from the blood stains on the porch – put there at the commission of the murder, prophesied the future connection of Mr. Smith to that murder?"

"I would say so, sir. I would say that in reality all the lives of men form but a very small link in the bigger chain of cosmic events, and I would say, in the life of man, the future is nothing, but the past unfolded. That is to say: we reap what we have sown. And if in the consciousness of man which is made up of his past and future, and is in his blood as an electric charge, could attach itself to negative plate such faces that appear on that plate would be either acknowledgments, or perhaps, projections of future events."

Pickard was motionless.

"So, in essence, you can predict the future?"

"I would say so if we understand we have access to our destiny."

"Sounds to me like what we shovel out of a stall. You say there was a woman's face?"

"Yes."

"And did you know the face?"

"It was not Mrs. Dean."

"Whose was it, then?"

"I didn't recognize the face."

"Then how do you know it wasn't Mrs. Dean?"

"Because it was a younger face."

"So you could make out a face, but couldn't recognize it?"

"Yes."

"Maybe it was a prophetic projection?" sneered Pickard.

"Or maybe it was Susan Henchman."

Pickard was angry at himself for falling into the trap.

Chapter Twenty

From The Department of Justice report on April 23, 1919.

Pickard then became a regular tool of the political ring of Keene which is in close touch with Concord.

Dr. Dekerlor worried about what The Department of Justice knew about him and his wife, Elsa Schiaparelli. He was concerned if The Department of Justice had information that could compromise him all his ambitions would be lost. Feri Weiss had to go to Worcester for several days, and when he returned home his wife told him,

"It was Sunday night when I came home with Lillian, and I had a funny sensation like someone was here. Then, I saw the muddy footprints on the carpet. I took Lillian upstairs with me, and locked our bedroom door, and barricaded it with a chair. She fell asleep, Thank God, and I lay down on the bed next to her. I lay there in the dark, and I was almost certain there was someone in the hall when I heard the chain for the electric light being pulled, and I see light under the door. I slowly get up, and go to the bureau, and take out the revolver, and drop the holster, which makes a noise. I was terrified. I heard a noise from Lillian's room, and then, the sound of a window being opened. I went over, and looked out our bedroom window, and saw Dekerlor run along the roof, then crouch down, and jump from the roof. When I was sure he was gone, I checked the house, and saw the papers on your desk were tampered with, and thought he must have been looking for some reports."

"I'm sorry he scared you like that. I'll be sure to talk to him about his manners, and remind him that only a coward would scare women and children. He won't like that much," said Feri.

"Why would he break into our house?"

"Oh, he's trying to find out what The Department knows about him and his wife, but I would think he'd be smart enough to know we don't keep intelligence in our houses."

"I would have shot him, Feri…"

Feri laughed.

"I know…I know…"

After the autopsy, Father Hennon talked to Valkenburgh and Weiss about a Grand Jury Hearing with the hope that Albany Pelletier would get to testify. The priest had a bad experience with Rich over a church deposit, and ended up taking the church account to a different bank. Rich found a six dollar discrepancy between the cash and deposit slip of a Monday morning deposit. He blamed the altar boy who brought the deposit to the bank, but the priest realized he'd miscounted the money. Rich didn't apologize to the altar boy or the priest which left a bad feeling. Roy Pickard didn't waver from his Mrs. Dean Killed Her Husband theory, and when asked to convene a Grand Jury, answered that there wasn't enough evidence to justify the cost to the taxpayers of Cheshire County. Valkenburgh and Weiss didn't have jurisdiction over the murder, the state and county officials did. The murder only had their attention if it was an act of espionage under The Espionage Act of 1917. Valkenburgh and Weiss were beginning to understand that Pickard was impeding the investigation after saying no to an autopsy, and again, to a Grand Jury, and his insistence that Mrs. Dean did it. Mrs. Dean died in the fall of 1919, and as far as Pickard was concerned that ended the investigation for him anyway. Father Hennon had a different opinion, and persuaded Valkenburgh and Weiss to his concern.

"I think we should go see Norman to figure out a way to bust this open," said Feri.

"He would know, wouldn't he?" said Valkenburgh.

"I don't know what to do," confessed Feri.

"Maybe we should ask Dr. Dekerlor?"

Feri laughed.

"We better ask quick before someone shoots him," he said.

Chapter Twenty-One

The two men traveled to Boston to meet with Norman Gifford. Again, Gifford was behind his wooden desk reading, and Valkenburgh and Weiss sat in straight-backed chairs with a belt and holster hanging on the back of Valkenburgh's chair, and a newspaper on the floor near him.

"I read this sad story about Ty Cobb's mother. Do you know anything about it?" asked Valkenburgh.

"What's that?" murmured Gifford while reading.

"I say, did you ever hear the story of how Ty Cobb's mother accidently shot his father?"

"Cobb's a helluva ballplayer though," mumbled Gifford.

"Why would she do that?" asked Feri.

"Cobb's old man was highly jealous, and was convinced his wife was cheating on him, and he spied on her when she was in the bedroom through a window, and one time, she saw him, and thought he was a burglar, and shot him with a pistol he gave her."

"Sounds Shakespearian," said Weiss.

"Helluva ballplayer," said Gifford.

"They say that's why he's so nasty because of his father."

"I would believe that."

"Helluva ballplayer."

Gifford returned to reading, and when he finished, he asked,

"In your opinion, the autopsy hasn't moved the investigation along?"

Valkenburgh and Weiss looked at each other.

"No," answered Weiss, "Pickard is still saying Mrs. Dean did it, and refuses to convene a Grand Jury to examine the evidence because they're afraid of a Catholic night watchman who saw Rich's horse at the time the horse was kicking Rich in the barn."

"Pickard is stifling the works?"

"The autopsy wouldn't have been done unless we did it," said Valkenburgh, "there's a petition in town asking the county officials for a Grand Jury Hearing, and it hasn't been signed by Bean and Symonds because they believe it will be a witch trial for Rich."

"Who's this nut that can see faces in photographs?"

"Dr. Dekerlor a highly controversial criminal psychologist."

"How did he get involved in this?"

"He was brought from New York by the victim's brother," said Weiss.

"I can't see where he's any help," said Gifford.

"Probably not, but he might just be nutty enough to be a help to those who don't want to look too closely at the evidence," speculated Valkenburgh.

The men were silent.

"All right," said Gifford, "our strategy is going to be to rattle those who are holding up the investigation into making a move of some kind. I say we go after some of Rich's fellow Masons, and see, if we can get them angry enough to make a move."

"How though?" asked Weiss.

"We interview them, and treat them like criminals. If my sense of Bean and Symonds is right, these men are community leaders who would be highly offended if they were treated as criminals. That's what we're going to do. It's a gamble, but we have to do something bold especially in a small town like this where everything is so tight. We're not interviewing Bean and Symonds, we're interrogating them, and purposefully trying to get them angry so they make a poorly thought out move is our hope. The other thing, of course, is surprise. We don't let them know we're coming so they're caught with their guard down."

Valkenburgh and Weiss looked at each other.

"I'll buy the tickets this afternoon," said Valkenburgh.

It was a Friday afternoon in March when unannounced the three agents walked into the office of Bean and Symonds. Gifford showed his badge to the young secretary.

"Department of Justice," he said, "we want to talk to Mr. Bean and Mr. Symonds."

Not intimidated, the young girl shot back,

"Do you have an appointment?"

"No."

"I would be happy to make one for you."

"Government business takes priority. We're not going to waste the time and resources to come back some other day. If you like, we can issue a search warrant and go through the whole place or you can quietly produce Mr. Bean and Mr. Symonds, and we can, with a minimum of interruption, conduct our business."

The young secretary looked like she'd been slapped in the face.

"One moment," she said. She stood up and walked into an office. After a good five minutes, the office door opened, and out came the young secretary with a man.

"Hello," he said, "I'm Delcie Bean." He shook the three men's hands as Valkenburgh made introductions. Another, taller man appeared who introduced himself as Merrill Symonds. Gifford and Bean went into his office, and Valkenburgh and Weiss went into Symonds's office. About half an hour later, the young secretary heard raised voices through Bean's office door, and not long after that, Agent Weiss came out of Symonds's office and went into Bean's. The young secretary felt tension, and when the agents left, neither Mr. Bean nor Mr. Symonds said a word.

Chapter Twenty-Two

From the Department of Justice report on March 21, 1919.

Mr. Symonds stated that there was a very strong feeling in town; that his own attitude had been misunderstood by many, and he was accused by some of attempting to shield a murderer, and to stifle the investigation. Under questioning, he repeatedly stated that he believed the only way to clear the atmosphere was to have a grand jury investigation..."

It didn't take long at all for the Gifford strategy to work; the next morning the desk clerk handed Valkenburgh a note which read: Come see me, Urgent. Mrs. Bryant. Valkenburgh and Weiss walked to the infirmary, and waited while Mrs. Bryant finished with a patient. When the door closed, she said,

"There's a secret meeting at a hotel in Winchendon at one."

"How did you find out about it, then?" asked Weiss.

"I was called to the Symonds's house last night for a child with a fever, and through a partially open door, I heard Mr. Symonds on the telephone; he was pretty angry."

"Do you know who he was talking to?"

"He asked the operator for Keene."

"Pickard?" guessed Weiss.

"Why are you telling us?" asked Valkenburgh.

"I didn't like the way they treated Mrs. Dean."

"How many hotels are there in Winchendon?" asked Weiss.

"Two."

"Thanks."

As they walked out of the infirmary, they realized they had no auto to drive to Winchendon, and Valkenburgh pointed to the library where the selectman's office was. They ran into Peter Hogan on the steps.

"If we left it with a full tank, could we borrow your auto?"

Hogan was confused by the unusual request.

"My auto? What on earth for?" he asked.

"We just got a tip, and we need to drive to Winchendon."

"Oh, yes, I see. A full tank would be fine. Watch the back passenger tire, it loses air."

"Thanks. We appreciate it," said Weiss.

"I parked behind the building. A Ford sedan," Hogan said.

It was at The Toy Town Tavern that the clerk told Valkenburgh and Weiss he had a reservation for a one o'clock from a man who called that morning from Jaffrey. Valkenburgh asked about the room next to the meeting room, and was able to get access. They went up to the adjoining room, and saw a doorway that connected the two rooms. Weiss went back down to the lobby, and hid behind a newspaper to watch who came in. Around one, Delcie Bean and Merrill Symonds came in, got the room number from the clerk, and climbed the stairs. Several more minutes went by, and Homer White and William Webster came in, followed, after a brief interval, by Roy Pickard and Sheriff Lord. Weiss went back to the room where Valkenburgh was listening through the door with a water glass. After twenty minutes, the men left the room.

"Looks like they're going to have a grand jury after all," said Valkenburgh.

Chapter Twenty-Three

Several days after the secret meeting it was announced by Roy Pickard there would be a County Grand Jury on the murder of Dr. Dean at the Keene Courthouse with Judge John Kivel presiding, with the State Attorney General, Oscar Young, and the County Prosecutor, Roy Pickard as the lawyers. Valkenburgh and Weiss got a message from Father Hennon who they went to see at the parish house. After the amenities, Valkenburgh and Weiss sat in chairs offered by the priest.

"I saw in the paper about the convening of a grand jury, and I wanted to share my concerns with someone who would be sympathetic."

"Of course, Father, please continue," said Weiss.

"I have doubts about Roy Pickard, and I want to see that Albany Pelletier is called to testify."

There was a long moment.

"I don't know what we can do about that," said Valkenburgh, "the county grand jury is not under our jurisdiction. We can ask that he be allowed to testify, but the decision is up to them."

The room was still until Weiss said,

"Wait a minute! What if The Department of Justice approaches Judge Kivel with a request to allow a Federal attorney to assist the county prosecutor on the grand jury? Our justification would be that if Dean was murdered as an act of espionage, and there was to be a Federal grand jury on espionage, we wouldn't have to duplicate our work from the murder trial?"

"Excellent, Feri," said Valkenburgh.

About a week before the start of the grand jury, Valkenburgh got an appointment to meet with Judge Kivel. Father Hennon and the Jaffrey selectmen came with Valkenburgh and Weiss. Valkenburgh could tell Judge Kivel wasn't in the mood for this. Weiss started,

"Your Honor, the Department of Justice would petition the court if Albany Pelletier would be allowed to testify before the grand jury?"

"Is that all?" asked the judge.

"No sir, I have another motion."

"Proceed."

"In the event of a Federal grand jury called on espionage matters, and the possibility of Dr. Dean's murder being an act of espionage, would you allow a Federal attorney to assist the county prosecutor in the county grand jury to prevent duplication?"

"No. Motion denied."

The judge recognized Father Hennon.

"Your Honor, I too, would ask the court to allow Albany Pelletier to testify as he is a humble man who could be easily overlooked in the excitement of a grand jury hearing. I too would ask for a Fed…"

"No. Motion denied."

Judge Kivel recognized William Coolidge who, once it was clear he was asking the same question over again, was cut off with,

"The State of New Hampshire doesn't need any help from outsiders. Good day, gentlemen."

Valkenburgh wired Norman Gifford the frustrating results of their interview with Judge Kivel. Gifford wired back,

Stake out the courthouse. NG.

Chapter Twenty-Four

From the Department of Justice report on April 17, 1919:

I was summoned as a witness before the Grand Jury at Keene. Before I testified, Mr. Pickard wanted to see me at his office...Now that I think it over, to this day, I still feel that he wanted me to think as he did, and answer questions the way he wanted before the Grand Jury, so that my impressions would be the same as his. This made me sick, and I left him.

Feri Weiss staked out the waiting room at the courthouse. When he needed to hide himself, he put the newspaper in front of his face. He was in the waiting room with the Colfelt women: Margaret, and her daughter, Natalye who were waiting to testify. Weiss was behind a newspaper when Lawyer Pickard and Attorney General Young came through the door from the hearing room. Colfelt was a serious suspect, and from the warm and friendly welcome the lawyers gave the women, it was obvious the women would not be made uncomfortable when they testified. Pickard and Young were embarrassed when Weiss dropped the newspaper, and they realized who was observing them. They quickly left the room.

Arthur Smith came to Keene to testify before the grand jury, and when he checked in at the courthouse, Sheriff Lord told him to go see Lawyer Pickard on Roxbury Street. Arthur followed the direction the sheriff gave him, and found the office on the second floor. The secretary asked him to have a seat. When Lawyer Pickard came to get Arthur, he took him to a storage room instead of his office. He offered Arthur a box to sit on.

"You called for this afternoon?" he asked.

"Yes."

"You nervous?"

"Yes."

"That's only natural. You there when the body was found?"

"Yes."

"That must have been a shock?"

"Yes."

"What was Mrs. Dean like?"

"What do you mean?"

"How was she acting?"

"Confused, scared."

"Like she'd done something terrible?"

Arthur looked at Pickard.

"No. She was confused about the whereabouts of her husband."

"She was the last person to see him alive, right?"

"Not necessarily. Someone could have come onto the farm."

Pickard was frustrated, and took a different tack.

"Did you ever see lights?"

"Sure."

"Probably automobile lights, wouldn't you say?"

"Autos have two lights, I only saw one."

"Maybe it was a star then?"

"Too close to the ground. Where I saw lights there were no houses or roads."

"What about around Dean farm?"

"I haven't seen them there, but I've been told by others they have."

"Where have you seen them?"

"From Temple Mountain and Monadnock."

"Really?"

"Yes."

Pickard looked away, and when he looked back, he asked,

"Who do you think did it?"

"Mr. Rich."

"You think a man as upstanding as Mr. Rich would commit murder?"

"Mr. Rich has a temper."

"I think Mrs. Dean did it. Don't you think Mrs. Dean did it, Arthur?"

"No, I don't."

"I think she was jealous of him paying attention to women in the village."

"It's easy to accuse Mrs. Dean now that she can't defend herself, isn't it?"

"I will be interviewing you this afternoon," curtly said Pickard.

Ed Baldwin was a friend, fellow Mason, and neighbor to Charles Rich. He was the Financial Secretary of the Masons and Rich was the treasurer. The two men had an arrangement where Baldwin let Rich use some of his land for a garden, and in return, Rich let Baldwin use his barn and horse and buggy. The night of the murder, Baldwin took Rich's horse and buggy out, and made a trip to Bean and Symonds to get bags of sawdust. During his testimony, Pickard asked him,

"What time did you get back to the barn?"

"I couldn't have taken – the trip might have taken – the way I would usually drive in there and out, which is just exercise for the mare, and I would have to leave the sawdust, might have been done in thirty minutes. Not over forty," answered Baldwin.

"What was the latest time you got back to Rich's house that night?"

"Couldn't have been later than 8:45."

"Could it have been nine?"

"No, sir. I couldn't have used that much time unless I had walked the mare, which I naturally wouldn't do if I was out to give her a little exercise."

"Was it as late as quarter to nine when you were at Bean and Symonds for the sawdust?"

"No, sir, I went to Bean and Symonds first."

"Supposing some person had said you were at Bean and Symonds at 8:45, just starting from there with the bag of sawdust, what would you say to that?"

"I wouldn't care to say very plainly just what I think of it."

"That you weren't there that late?"

"I wasn't there at that time, no, sir."

"Is there any doubt about that in your mind?"

"There is none, no, sir."

From the Department of Justice report on December 13, 1918.

Q. On the evening of August 13th of this year, do you remember what time it was when the horse kicked you?

A. It was very near 9 o'clock, before or a little after.

Q. What time did Dr. Dean arrive at your home that night?

A. It was pretty soon afterwards, because I was heating some water to bathe my face. I wanted to get some hot water on it. I just started the electric heater in the kitchen when I saw him driving up the road. I remember it was 9 o'clock because I was weary and wanted to get up early the next morning.

It turned out that Pickard and Young used Valkenburgh to help minimize the influence of Albany Pelletier's testimony on the grand jury. Albany was the third to last witness to testify before the jury which didn't allow much time for the jury to consider his testimony, and Valkenburgh, who generated a lot more attention than a night watchman from Jaffrey, testified after Albany which overshadowed what Albany said. Pickard asked Albany,

"Were you on duty there the night of August 13 last?"

"Yes."

"Did you see Mr. Rich's horse that night?"

"Yes."

Where?"

"Right down there by the sawdust chute."

"What time was this you saw him?"

"Nine o'clock at night I saw him. Yes. I go around every hour. I go once every hour with that clock. As I go around every hour, you know, I went at nine, and I would go again at ten o'clock, as you know."

Several hours later the jury returned the verdict:

Murder by Person or Persons Unknown.

Epilogue

In the hundred years since the murder was committed, it is believed this is an unsolved murder. The verdict of the Grand Jury became the explanation of the crime. There are two important documents to get a sense of what happened, and they are: *Hearing by the Grand Jury on the Death of William K. Dean.* Transcribed and Published by Margaret C. Bean, and the *Department of Justice reports* written by the agents released to Margaret Bean under the Freedom of Information Act. In order to grasp the scope of what happened one must look at both, and this is where it gets conflicted. Margaret Bean, the daughter in law of Delcie Bean, was the first person to read the Department of Justice reports, and in a speech to the Amos Fortune Forum in July of 1989 said,

"I read the Department of Justice files, and find nothing there of importance that is not brought out in the Grand Jury Inquest. This is both reassuring and disappointing, because I had hoped to find the answer...that it had been espionage, or counter-espionage, or that there had been enough evidence against Lawrence Colfelt, or some guilty person, and the government had resolved the case. But, no!"

Now I'll excerpt part of a Department of Justice

report written on April 23, 1919, the day after the verdict of the Grand Jury, written by Feri Weiss.

"If there ever was any miscarriage of justice, it was before this Grand Jury. I had the good chance to observe the intimate and friendly relations between Mr. Pickard and Attorney General Young on the one hand, and the Colfelt family, on the other. As I was in the waiting room, in the Court House, unnoticed by these two officials, when they greeted the Colfelts. It is clear that the Attorney General, as well as the County Solicitor, and perhaps even Judge Kivel, are in a conspiracy to whitewash the suspects, namely, Rich and Colfelt.

The fact that the Judge, prompted by the Attorney General and by the County Solicitor, refused to have a U.S. Attorney present at the Grand Jury hearing, as an assistant to the attorney general, is proof enough for me that my above statement in regard to this conspiracy is true.

It is the Agent's sincere hope that a Federal Grand Jury will be convened so that this case will get the attention it deserves, and not be put off by the trickeries of unscrupulous officials and politicians."

One more final observation. On a visit to the Conant Cemetery in Jaffrey to visit the grave of Charles Rich, I was struck by the discovery that Charles, Lana, and Georgiana are buried together. Charles died in 1933, Lana in 1938, and Georgiana in 1955, and didn't live in Jaffrey.

They were the only ones to know how Charles got his black eye.

THE DEATH OF DR. DEAN

About the Author

Jack Coey lives in Keene, NH.